2 5053 00672155 9

WITHDRAWN HEDBERG LIBRARY

GIFT OF

John Warren Stewig

Carthage

D1055382

Other novels by Mary Stolz

The Explorer of Barkham Street
Cat Walk
What Time of Night Is It?
Go and Catch a Flying Fish
Cider Days
Ferris Wheel
The Edge of Next Year
Lands End
By the Highway Home
A Wonderful, Terrible Time
The Noonday Friends
The Mystery of the Woods
The Bully of Barkham Street
A Dog on Barkham Street

For Younger Readers

Emmett's Pig
(An I Can Read Book)

The Scarecrows and Their Child

Cur
PZ
7
S875854
Sc
1987

MARY STOLZ

The Scarecrows
and
Their Child

with drawings by Amy Schwartz

Harper & Row, Publishers

HEDBERG LIBRARY
CARTHAGE COLLEGE
KENOSHA, WISCONSIN

The Scarecrows and Their Child
Text copyright © 1987 by Mary Stolz
Illustrations copyright © 1987 by Amy Schwartz
Printed in the U.S.A. All rights reserved.

Library of Congress Cataloging-in-Publication Data
Stolz, Mary, date
    The scarecrows and their child.

    Summary: While looking for employment, two
scarecrows become separated from their cat child,
finding each other again on Halloween.
    [1. Scarecrows—Fiction.   2. Halloween—Fiction.
3. Parent and child—Fiction.   4. Fantasy]
I. Schwartz, Amy, ill.   II. Title.
PZ7.S875854Sc 1987   [E]   87-115
ISBN 0-06-026007-6
ISBN 0-06-026008-4 (lib. bdg.)

Typography by Constance Fogler
1 2 3 4 5 6 7 8 9 10

For

BETTY AND WALTER BAUGHMAN,

Next-Door Dears

(M.S.)

For KAREN

(A.S.)

The Scarecrows and Their Child

One

Two scarecrows had worked on a New England farm for many years without meeting. She was in berries and garden vegetables, he was in field corn, and except for one night a year—which the farmer did not know about—they got no time off.

A child, long since grown old, had named the corn scarecrow Handforth. He was called Handy, for short. The garden scarecrow was named Blossom, because when she was built the farmer's wife said she was as pretty as a flower.

Blossom was plump and had a sweetly cheerful cotton face. She wore a bonnet, cotton gloves, and a calico dress. She was stuffed with straw. Handy was made of sterner stuff—a wooden crossbar. His head was a pail with a serious face painted on it.

Blossom thought Handy cut a fine figure in his tattered tailcoat, white gloves, and long plaid scarf. She especially liked to see him when the corn had been harvested and he stood alone in the field, tall and skinny against the autumn sky. For his part, Handy considered Blossom the very picture of beauty and kindness and cozy charm.

But except for peeks exchanged over the pasture fence, they remained strangers. They had not even met at Hallowe'en, that one night of the year when all scarecrows leave their posts and foregather with witches, goblins, ghosts, wraiths, and the like to revel and riot in a huge assembly ball.

Each year, Blossom waited modestly for him to seek her out, and each year he was too bashful to do so. It seemed, therefore, that they would go no further than increasingly fond glances.

However.

It came to pass that for one reason or another, all of them sad and too bad, the farm was abandoned. Away went the farmer, the farmer's wife, their children, their flocks and herds. In the fields no corn was planted, and the old brown stubble rotted into the earth. The farm garden grew weedy and wild. Rhubarb and strawberries and asparagus

(4)

came up on their rangy own and went to seed. Burdocks and ragwort sprouted and flourished. Ivy crept up the farmhouse steps, over the porch, under the doors. It pried through cracks in the windows, pushed into the eaves, trailed across the floors of empty rooms.

Years passed. The roof sagged. Rain found crevices to seep through. The big red barn, which had been for so long so neat and so snug, began to lean and to leak.

During all this time, Handy and Blossom remained steadfast in their appointed places. Work—guarding garden and corn field—was their job, their mission to be alone and watchful. They had been diligent scarecrows since the day they were made, and they could not understand, as the years went by, this desertion by the human beings who had made them and put them there—in the field, in the garden.

As the farmer had not thought to explain to these helpers that the land no longer supported him and his family, they could only feel abandoned and misused.

"Useless and lonely," said Handy to himself, his scarf flapping in the wind, his tin pail rattling. He looked across the wide field to where Blossom stood behind the fence in the deserted garden, the ribbons on her bonnet fluttering, her sweet cotton face wistful as she gazed back at him.

He stared about at empty acres that had known neither planting nor harvest for more years than he could now recollect and said to himself that to remain on point duty when there was no longer any point to the duty was something not even the most dutiful of Yankee scarecrows could be relied upon to do forever.

Perhaps I should retire, he thought, his gaze still fixed upon Blossom.

Retire! What a dazzling idea! What was to keep him from her now? Who could keep him at his lonely post if he decided to leave it?

"I'll do it!" he said, and with a mighty tug hauled himself out of the earth where he'd stood, a sturdy sentinel, all the days and nights of his life. He started across the fields. He came to a gate in the crooked, sagging fence.

He stopped.

Suppose—suppose she didn't *want* him to speak to her after all this time? Suppose she considered him a crude and rough-hewn fellow not worthy of

her dainty self, and the first words he heard from
her were, "Go away"?

He half turned back. He'd been solitary his
whole life long. He could face the rest of it alone.
Looking over his shoulder for a good-bye glance at
her, he saw that her pretty painted face was filled
with alarm. Her eyes seemed to be pleading with
him.

Suppose that after all she *did* want him to speak?

His wooden heart thumped, and— "I must
know," he said to himself. Knocking down the

cockeyed gate that hung from the fence, he marched straight up to Blossom where she stood wide-eyed in a rough patch of rhubarb.

Overcome with shyness, he bowed stiffly and said in a hollow voice, "I am called Handforth," and waited for her dismissal.

"You're called Handy," she said in just the gentle voice he had always known she would have. "I'm so happy that you changed your mind."

"Changed my mind?"

"You were going to go away without speaking. But you spoke, and I am very glad."

"You *are?*" he said, wanting to take her in his arms, but unwilling to seem forward.

"My name is Blossom."

"Oh, I know," he declared passionately. "I have heard your name on the breeze, and in the songs of birds, and in the crackle of starlight...."

"Oh, my," she murmured.

They looked at each other in happy silence, and then Handy got down on one splintered knee. "Miss Blossom, I love you."

"I know that," she said. "I love you, too."

"Then—will you marry me?"

"Of course."

Hand in hand, they walked out of the garden, uphill to a little cherry and apple orchard where now only wild creatures—deer and birds, skunks and raccoons—fed on the fruits that still grew there.

Under a tangle-boughed cherry tree they exchanged their vows and then went to set up housekeeping in the barn, in a horse stall directly under a part of the roof that didn't leak.

Two

For a season, this pair of hard workers took life easy, rejoicing in their freedom to move about at will. They walked over the hills and pastures, chatting comfortably with their neighbors—crows and deer, raccoons, the occasional fox.

At night, after the barn owl who lived in the rafters had left for the fields, they settled in the straw and had long talks.

"Did They ever explain to you why They went and left us all alone?" he asked one day.

Both knew who "They" were.

"No," she said. "Not a word. They didn't even say good-bye."

"How strange. After we'd worked so hard for them. I wonder what happened."

"There was a foreclosure."

"Oh. I see." After a moment, he asked, "What's a foreclosure?"

"I don't know."

"I see," he said again, though he did not. Still, it no longer seemed important.

They had time to observe much that they had been too busy to notice before.

"How pretty the swallows are, twittering and twirling," said Blossom.

"How dainty the rain sounds, pattering on the roof," said her husband.

So the months passed in happy companionship.

Then one evening as they sat outside the barn, watching the sun go down behind the purple hills, Blossom leaned close to her husband and whispered, "Handforth—we are going to have a baby."

"Oh, how wonderful," he said, taking her in his wooden embrace. "How very grand and wonderful."

In a while, the baby was born.

"It's a boy!" said Handy.

"It's a cat!" said Blossom.

They were not surprised that their child was a black kitten. Scarecrows never know what kind of offspring they are going to have...a chicken, a piglet, a field mouse. Now and then another little scarecrow, though this is rare. They frequently have a cat child.

Blossom and Handy were devoted to their son, whom they named Bohel. They played with him, crooned to him, protected him from dangers that did not exist, tried to protect him from those that did. They told him bedtime stories about druids and goblins and Puss-in-Boots. His mother kept his fur tidy with a little comb she'd found on the barn floor. His father undertook to teach him how to climb trees. Handy had never climbed a tree himself, but he realized that this was part of a cat's training and did his best to instruct without actually setting an example. Bohel, who preferred to groom himself and knew about climbing from the day he was born, did not complain about these attentions. He was a sweet, affectionate child. They were so proud of him, took such pleasure in his frisky ways, that it seemed life could offer no greater bounty.

It is true that he caused them anxiety. He thought nothing of springing up to the loft and racing along the high beams. He teased the barn owl, who had long talons and a testy disposition. Now and then the owl swooped at him, and Handy and Blossom would gaze upward in terror. But

Bohel, with a flick of his tail, always skittered out of reach.

Sometimes he went out in the evening and did not return until morning. Blossom and Handy would stay awake, wondering where he'd gone, worrying about this small kitten out in the night where owls and raccoons and foxes were on the prowl. Then, when they heard him come leaping lightly home, Blossom would sigh and say. "He got home this time, Handy, but who knows tomorrow? You must speak to him."

Therefore, "Where *have* you been?" Handy would demand gruffly of his son.

"Going up and down," Bohel would say brightly. "Racing round and round."

"Bohel, you make your mother and me very uneasy. We fear for you."

"I'm sorry, Father," the kitten would say truly. "I won't do it again."

Of course he did it again.

The scarecrows decided there was nothing to do but wait and hope that Bohel's good cat sense, of which he had enough to awe them, would keep him safe from harm.

Saturday was the big tidying-up day. First they fluffed and patted their straw living room and dusted their shelf. Then Blossom stuffed herself with fresh straw, of which there was a lot still in the barn. She brushed her cotton face, smoothed her calico dress, flicked the ribbons of her bonnet. Handy polished his tin pail head, shook out his tailcoat and scarf, clapped his gloves together.

Then they turned their attention to Bohel, combed him, peered in his ears, smoothed his whiskers, made sure there were no thistles or burrs in his tail. Bohel squirmed but did not protest.

One Saturday in the early fall, Handy said, "Well, what now?"

Blossom and Bohel looked at him in perplexity.

"I mean," he said, "every Saturday we get all slicked up and then don't do anything *about* it."

"What should we do?" Blossom asked in a bewildered voice.

Bohel licked his chest and looked away. He was content with the way things were.

"Actually and in fact," Blossom went on thoughtfully, "we don't do anything about it the rest of the week either."

"Until Hallowe'en, of course," Handy said,

sounding happy once more. "Then we surely do something about something."

"What's Hallowe'en?" asked Bohel.

His parents exchanged glances. "No," said Blossom. "We are not going to tell you about that just yet."

"We're saving it, for a wonderful surprise," said Handy.

"Well, that's nice," said Bohel, who wasn't fond of surprises. Usually they made his fur stand on end. "I don't mind if you wait."

"There is still the problem of our day-to-day existence," said Handy.

"Why is it a problem?" Blossom asked plaintively. "What is wrong with the way our life is now? Oh, Handy—are you getting bored with us, with Bohel and me?"

"Of *course* not," he said, holding her close. "Get up on my shoulder here, son. There, we're all together. How could I be bored when I have such a wonderful family?"

"Then why did you say—*what now?*"

"Well. Well, I don't truly know, Blossom, my dear. Perhaps I miss the challenge of work. Both of us worked all our lives in true New England scarecrow fashion, and now we do little but listen to the rain and the birds and take care of Bohel, who seems too able to take care of himself."

"Then, in a way, you are bored," she said in a sad voice.

Handy took up his pipe—a corncob he'd found in the meadow—and considered the idea. He did not smoke but found holding the pipe a comfort when he wanted to think. "I wonder. Blossom, you must know that I could never tire of life with you and our lovely boy. But consider this—are we setting Bohel a good example? He may come to think life is of no more weight than a pod of milk-weed floss."

"That's how I like to think of it," said Bohel. "Everything's silky the way it is."

"You see?" Handy said to his wife. "He doesn't know about real life."

"It seems real enough to me," Bohel said. "We stay together, and laugh, and look out for each other—and isn't that real?"

"It is, it is," said Handy. "But aside from being happy, we don't *do* anything."

"Well, but what do you want to do?" Bohel asked. "What *can* you do?"

"The answer is clear," said his father. "Your mother and I must go to work again. I fear we are not cut out for the leisured life. Work is in our bones. That is to say, it's deep in your mother's straw and ingrained in me."

Bohel looked at them and sighed. "Well, it's been a very happy time, the three of us together all the day and—" He stopped, not wanting to draw their attention to nights. "It's been lovely, and I don't see why it has to change. Do you, Mother?"

But Blossom said, "I am afraid your father and I were not meant to be idle." Anyway, she whispered to herself, *Handy* wasn't meant to be, or thinks he wasn't meant to be, and if he is going to start looking for work, my place is at his side.

Three

So a new regime began.

Every morning Handy and Blossom went forth and looked for work. While they were gone, Bohel took care of things at home. With his claws he dug up root vegetables in their little garden and pulled out the wicked witch grass that grew there. He swept the stall floor with his tail. After a little tom-foolery for relaxation—leaping and scampering; chasing crickets, leaves, his tail; jumping at shadows—he groomed himself and then took cat naps off and on.

Now he was the bored one—alone all day with only that sleepy owl to tease. No creatures came into the barn that he could visit with. Mice avoided him. The deer and the foxes stayed far away. There were raccoons nearby, but they were rowdies and Bohel was a little afraid of them. He was just as glad they left him alone. The farm, which had never seemed to him lonely before, was sad and empty without his parents' presence.

And, alas.

Evening after evening Handy and Blossom returned to the barn discouraged, exhausted, and unemployed.

Bohel was a canny cat who loved his parents dearly. Since they insisted that work was what they needed, he wished to help them in any way that he could. Perhaps they had been out of the world too long and did not remember how to communicate with people. He had never, his own self, met a human person, but knew he'd have no trouble communicating with one if he chose to.

Any cat knew how to do that. If he chose to.

When several weeks had gone by in the unsuccessful job hunt, he asked his father and mother what they said to the farmers when they asked for work.

Handy and Blossom looked at him in alarm.

"Say to them?" Blossom gave a rustling sigh. "Oh, Bohel—you don't understand. We can never associate with human beings again. The ones we had went off and left us in the lurch without a by-your-leave. I don't mean to sound resentful, but facts are facts."

"How can you get a job if you won't ask for one?" said Bohel.

"I do not wish to see a human being again," said Handy. "Much less do I wish to *ask* one for anything."

(23)

"Why?" asked his son.

"But we just explained that!"

"You said that those farmers went off and left you behind. That doesn't mean that all human beings would be unkind. Besides, maybe they had a reason."

"The foreclosure," said Blossom and Handy together.

"What's that?" Bohel asked.

"We don't know, but they had one. Maybe that was the reason," Blossom said, adding, "Just the same, they could have said good-bye."

"But if you don't ask the farmers for work," Bohel insisted, "what do you do, when you go out every day? Who *do* you ask?"

"Oh, my goodness," Blossom said. "We inquire of other scarecrows, of course. Of farm animals. Anyone who might know of a vacancy coming up."

"But if there is already a scarecrow at work where you're asking, how can you get a job if he's got it?"

"We think," Handy said stiffly, "that this time we will take a distant post—in meadows and pastures, fens, and the like."

Bohel ran a paw over his face. Then he said,

"Father, I think that probably people don't care if there are birds in meadows and pastures, or in fens. Maybe only human beings can give employment to scarecrows, and if you won't go near them, that's why you can't find work."

"You know, son," said Handy, "there are times when you give me a pain in the pail."

Four

"Just the same," Handy said to his wife as they crossed the fields the following morning, "Bohel has put his paw on the crux of the matter."

"You mean—"

"I mean that no one is going to hire us to scare birds in distant pastures. And we shall never get work by asking our fellow scarers. Bohel is right. As usual," he added irritably. He sighed till his tin head rattled. "We shall have to go to the farmers themselves."

"Now? Today?"

"We'll strike while our dander is up."

"But Handy—my dander is down."

"Nevertheless, dear—it's the only thing to do. We shall apply at the next farmhouse, at the kitchen door. Face to face with the farmer."

"Or his wife."

"Or his wife. Of course."

"I don't want to face either one."

"Nor do I. Still—take heart, Blossom. We are together!"

After a mile or so they came to a prosperous-looking farmstead and marched through the garden, up to the back door. Frost was already on the pumpkins—except for two big ones that had been converted to jack-o'-lanterns and were standing at attention on the bottom step.

Handy saluted them. "I see you fellows are all set for Hallowe'en," he said heartily. When the jacks did not reply, he said sternly, "We're looking for work. You can at least say if there's any chance of a job around here."

The jack-o'-lanterns grinned but said nothing.

"Think they're hot stuff because they light up at night," Handy said, deeply embarrassed. Imagine being snubbed by a pumpkin, he thought. And in front of Blossom. It's mortifying. He sighed right through his whole frame. "Well, let's go, Blossom dear."

Bracing themselves, the scarecrows stumped up the back porch steps to the kitchen door. Handy

knocked on it soundly, and in a moment the farmer's wife appeared, looking down as she wiped floury hands on her apron.

"Madam," said Handy, "I am a husky scarecrow in good condition, and this is my lovely wife, who works with me. We wish to hire out as a couple and are here to inquire about a possible position in—"

The woman looked up and began to scream. "Help! Police! Robbers!"

The farmer came charging into the room with a shotgun. The woman fainted on the floor. The

farmer jumped over her. "Who are you, you ruffians?" he shouted. "Wait till Hallowe'en to pull your nutty stunts! Get! *Get!* Or I'll fill you full of buckshot!"

He shot over their heads.

Stumbling, bumping into each other, the farmer's angry voice pursuing them, the two scarecrows ran down the road and across a field as fast as they could.

Far away, under a tree beside a brook, they

rested while Blossom's straw settled and Handy got his pail on straight. Then, without a word, they started for home and their cozy horse stall and their loving son, Bohel.

As soon as he saw them, Bohel knew there'd been trouble.

"What happened?" he said. "Mother? Father? Did something terrible happen to you? Please tell me."

"No, no, no," said Blossom, pushing her bonnet back. "It's all been too much.... I can't speak of it."

"I guess we made a mistake," said Handy, "in talking to human beings. Any scarecrow worth his tatters should know better than to walk and talk when they're around." He clutched his pipe for reassurance and added, "Except on Hallowe'en, of course."

"Why then?" asked Bohel, who was getting more and more curious about this mysterious *Hallowe'en*. "What's different then?"

"Everything is different!" Handy said, tossing his scarf in the air. "Even for human beings. On that night, all the people dress themselves up to look like us—they pretend to be scarecrows and skeletons and witches and ghosts and cats and suchlike. Hallowe'en gives them an excuse to put on masks and act carefree in the streets. How are they to know if we mingle in the crowds with them?"

"Oh, golly!" Bohel exclaimed. "Hallowe'en must be fun for them."

"Not nearly the fun it is for us," said Blossom.

"*Tell* me!" said Bohel, who felt he'd waited long enough and now wanted to know the surprise, even if it made his fur rise.

Blossom clasped her gloves together and smiled. "How to begin, how to begin? Well, dear son, you must know that once a year there is the feast of Hallowe'en, and *everyone* observes it. Human beings, as we said, dress up to look like us and go out in the streets to beg—"

"Why?"

"It's part of the rite. If they didn't beg, the rite would be ruined, and that would be terrible."

"Unthinkable," said Handy.

"But what do *we* do?" Bohel asked. "We don't have to dress up or go begging, do we?"

"Of course not," said Handy. "We already *are* witches and scarecrows and ghosts and so forth, and you're a cat. *They* are just pretending. No, we go to a great gathering on the hill—and there we dance and sing and whirl around the bonfire.... Oh, we revel and raise a rumpus, let me tell you! It's a party such as you've never been to in your life—"

"I've never been to one at all," Bohel pointed out.

"Well, in a few days, you'll attend your very first revel. Then you'll see what you'll see—"

"Meanwhile," said Blossom, "I think we should forget about job hunting for a while."

"At least until after Hallowe'en," said Bohel, smoothing his whiskers and lashing his tail. He felt fizzy with anticipation.

"Yes, we'll wait till then," Handy said with relief.

They were silent for a while, and then Blossom said dreamily, "How the leaves twist and twirl as they fall to earth."

"How the geese call as they fly over the fields," said Handy with a gentle smile.

"How peaceful it is here in the evening," purred Bohel, thinking about Hallowe'en, happily confident that it would *not* be peaceful at all.

Five

The next morning the scarecrows got a job.

It was not one they'd asked for, looked for, or wanted. They got it because they were afraid to talk to the people who hired them.

They were sitting together, leaning against the barn, discussing their plans for Hallowe'en, now only a few nights away. Handy was holding his pipe. Blossom was examining an old pot holder she'd found. It was nice and squashy. Bohel was busy chasing leaves around the garden.

Into this calm drove a pair of human beings in a pickup truck. It was a young couple who had been to a country auction where they'd bought an old sleigh with rusty runners and a worn, cracked red leather seat.

As they parked near the barn, Handy whispered. "Be *very* still, my dear."

"You don't have to tell me," Blossom said in a shaky voice.

"Philip!" the young woman exclaimed, jumping from the truck. "Isn't this too marvelous? An old deserted farm! Maybe some wonderful things have been left behind. Oh, look! Look there at those two scarecrows! Oh, we simply must have them! Come *on*, Philip—help me get them into the truck. We'll put them in the sleigh on the lawn, and they'll be the *hit* of our Hallowe'en party!"

"Oh, my goodness," said Blossom. "Handforth, what shall we *do*?"

"Hush! They are coming over. Not a word, now."

The young woman ran at them, tugging her husband, shrieking with delight. It was too much for the scarecrows. They toppled against each other in terror.

"How do you suppose that happened?" said the woman. "There isn't a breath of air."

"Probably," said her husband, "they gave up the ghost." He chuckled. To the scarecrows it was a frightful sound.

The man leaned over and picked up Blossom. "Light as a feather. You grab him. He's just a couple of crossbars and a pail."

"Don't forget his pipe. It's too perfect! And her grubby little pot holder. The dear *things*! We'll say that they're married."

"What does she mean, she'll *say* we're married?" Blossom whispered as she was toted toward the truck.

"Hush, hush," said Handy, riding on the woman's shoulder.

"*Bohel!*" moaned Blossom.

"My son!" Handy cried mournfully, and he
called out, "We'll try to get back to you! Don't give
up hope...."

"Did you *hear* something?" the woman asked
her husband.

"No. Let's get going before someone sees us."

Bohel came around a corner of the barn just in time to see the truck drive off. He'd been after a mouse he hadn't caught, and only now did he hear his parents' cries.

"What's happening?" he called out. "Where are you going? Wait for me!"

"Bohel!" came his mother's anguished call, and "My son!" his father's fading voice.

He ran after them but was left behind in the dust of the speeding truck.

Six

Bohel ran after the truck where he'd seen his parents sprawling and calling until he could no longer follow its dust trail. Then he fell by the roadside, panting, the pads of his feet hot and aching, his mind spinning with bewilderment.

Where had they gone on that awful truck, and what should he do now? How to begin to find them?

What would he do without them?

Abruptly, he got to his feet and ran back to the farm, thinking that perhaps by some confusing chance the truck had returned. Or that he'd imagined the whole thing....

That's it, he said to himself. It was some awful sort of imagining I had—because they would never go away in a truck or in anything else and leave *me* behind.

Breathless, he sped up the road to home.

No truck. But perhaps it had brought them back and then gone its way?

He ran all around the barn, tore through the garden, raced into the horse stall, calling to them.

"Mother! Father! Please, please...where are you?" he mewed, his voice small in the vastness of the great barn.

Nobody. Nothing. His mother's pot holder wasn't there, or his father's pipe, and for some reason that made him believe that they were really gone.

He lay down in the straw and put his nose in his paws.

One thing he knew—some things were possible, some things were not. That his parents, for any reason, at any time, would go away and leave him alone was impossible. So—they had been abducted. They were gone, maybe never to return, and he didn't know what to do.

"I'm only a *kitten*," he said to himself. "I shouldn't be by *myself* this way." His parents had told him that one day he'd be a grown cat and would then want to leave them, go off into the world on his own. He hadn't believed them then,

didn't believe them now. Anyway, he was not a grown cat.

"I'm just a kitten," he whispered again. "I need my mother and father...."

For the next couple of days he wandered, listless, lonely, in and around the barn that had been his home. It did not feel like home now. He thought about his parents, their kindness, their courage. He yearned for the cozy evenings of talk and friendly silences that he had known since birth.

He abandoned the little garden he'd been getting ready for spring planting. Let the weeds grow. He roved the fields, now and then catching a mouse. Even a lonely cat gets hungry.

He slept a lot and had bad dreams.

One night a storm came trampling over the hills in an army of clouds and thunder and drenching rain. Bohel, curled in the straw, listened to the wind as it tore the last leaves from the trees, once sending a branch crashing earthward. He listened to the rain that drummed on the tin roof high above him and splashed in the yard beyond the open barn door.

"Mother?" he mewed. "Father?"—his voice lost in the whistling gale.

Seven

Days passed.

One morning, when he was lying in the horse stall, dozing, a raspy voice said, "Going to the party?"

Bohel leaped into the air, came down spitting, back arched, fur lifting lightly, ears laid back, eyes wild.

A broom was leaning against the barn door, looking very long and skinny against the morning light. He was an old broom with a worn-down brush so uneven that he couldn't stand straight.

"Where did *you* come from?" Bohel demanded.

"I fell off the back of my truck last night, and I've been poking around ever since, trying to find somebody to talk to."

Bohel's fur smoothed. He subsided, folding his paws under his chest. "Your truck?" he said. "Was there a pair of scarecrows in it?" he inquired eagerly.

"No. No scarecrows. Just the usual junk. I've been faithful to that family since I was knee-high to a whisk broom. But they were going to take me to the town dump." He gave a dismal sigh. "*That's* the end of the road, friend. No one who goes there ever returns."

Bohel caught his breath. Still—there'd be no reason to kidnap his parents only to take them to the town dump. He breathed again.

"But then," the chatty broom was going on, "the man decided I'd be good enough for the truck. So that's what I've been doing of late... sweeping up chips and straw and pebbles and junk from the back of the truck. Better than the dump, and all I'm good for anymore, I guess. But last night I fell off. Probably just as well. Probably I'm not good enough even for the truck," he said in a hollow voice. "I'm a washed-out old besom, that's all there is to it."

"Surely not," Bohel murmured politely, though to speak the truth, this was a sorry-looking fellow

and awfully sorry for himself. "What did you say about a party?" he asked, trying to turn the talk along cheerier lines.

"The Hallowe'en party, of course. It's tonight. over yonder." The broom inclined his head with a sudden motion that made him stagger. "If you don't mind," he said, "I'll come in and lie down. I've had a terrible night."

"Of course, of course," Bohel said kindly. "Can I get you something? A bean? A potato?"

"Maybe later," said the broom, cautiously lowering himself onto the straw. "I must rest first. I *must* get to the party. This may be," he added, close to tears, "my last revel-and-riot."

"Oh, but Broom!" Bohel cried out, understanding suddenly flashing upon him. "Broom! You must take me with you! I have lost my mother and father, and maybe there I can find—Broom? Are you listening to me. Please?"

But the broom was fast asleep.

All morning and most of the afternoon, Bohel was in and out of the barn, impatiently waiting for the broom to rouse himself. He did not think of disturbing the poor fellow's sleep but was determined to find out how to get to the party. If there was any way to manage it, his parents would get to it, too. He was sure of that.

"That's where I'll find them," he kept saying to himself, as he patrolled the barn and yard, stopping frequently to stare at the broom.

At last, when for the dozenth time he'd padded in on silent paws and stood gazing upon the skinny sleeper, the broom awoke. It was late afternoon. The stall was in shadow now, the sun slanting over the far side of the barn. Almost time for it to begin a final plunge behind the hills. Time for the owl to take off. Dying katydids were playing their last tunes in the brown and withered grass. An October breeze was throwing dust devils across the yard.

"Well," he said to the broom. "You're awake."

"Just about," answered the broom, struggling up and leaning, slightly canted, against the stall wall. "That did me a world of good. I feel like a new broom. I'll take that bean now, if you don't mind."

Bohel pointed to the shelf where he had arranged a piece of potato, a bean, and a sprig of leftover parsley.

"How thoughtful," said his guest. "You are a well-mannered young feline. Am I to have the

honor of meeting your parents?"

"I *told* you. They're gone."

"You're an orphan?"

"No! They got taken away in a truck. They'd been looking for work, but even if they'd found a job, they'd never leave me behind. Not ever. They're scarecrows," he added proudly.

"Excellent parents, scarecrows. Known for it. Well, they'll surely be at the party, come what may—or should I say, come what did. There's not a scarecrow would miss the Hallowe'en coven."

"Coven?"

"Yes, the *coven*," said the broom impatiently, a bit of parsley stuck to the corner of his mouth. "Don't you know *anything*? The gathering of us Hallowe'en revel-and-rioters."

"How do you get there?"

"*I* fly, of course." He added, "I had a witch, but she got away. She flew with me on Hallowe'en for years."

"How did she get away?"

"Maybe I didn't put that exactly right. She *left* me last year. Left me for a—" He broke off, sniffling.

"For a new broom?" Bohel said carefully.

"Yes," snapped the old broom.

"So you've always had someone to go with, until now."

"That's the sad and unvarnished truth."

"Could I go with you instead?"

The broom brightened. "Now there *is* an idea. There are, of course, all manner of cats that come to the coven. You'll be especially welcome, being black. You can ride on my back, the way my witch used to. Actually, I'd be better off with you. You'll be much lighter than she was. Oh boy, I hope she *sees* me with you. That'd show her—"

Bohel, growing impatient, said, "When do we go?"

"On the stroke of twelve. Midnight."

"That'll just give me time to tidy up."

Holding his tail down with both paws, he began to groom himself. Now he was sure—absolutely *sure*—that he was going to find his mother and father again, and he wished to be a credit to them at the Hallowe'en revel-and-riot.

Eight

The moon, round and gleaming, white as a bone, had lifted herself free of the dark tangle of branches in the orchard, when the broom, who had been standing in the barn doorway looking into the night, turned to the kitten and said, *"Now!"*

Bohel leaped, as he'd been instructed, to the broom's back, dug his claws into the tattered brush, and prepared for flight.

Off they went!

Streaking like a spear through the crisp peppery air, the broom headed for the far hills, Bohel clinging fast as the wind blew his fur and his whiskers back.

All around, the night was filled with party-goers.

Jack-o'-lanterns with lighted grins hurtled like comets past skeletons and milky ghosts. Demons and ghouls howled, spinning like dervishes in midair. Witches leaned over their brooms, beating them with little whips, urging them on with wild screams.

Far, far below, hundreds of scarecrows rushed across the moonlit fields.

On, on!

All at once the broom leveled off and shot earthward toward a wild, wide secret plateau in the middle of the foresty hills where Hallowe'en roisterers were assembling.

The broom headed toward a swirling throng that was making for a great bonfire in the center of the clearing. Shadows leaped and lengthened and shrank as the company danced and cavorted around the blaze. Sparks flew skyward to the moon, where she raced in and out of frayed clouds, and everywhere stars sprang and shot about like popcorn.

Bohel, dizzy with excitement, dug his claws tighter into the broom, for fear of falling and being trampled by phantoms and apparitions. The broom went leaping joyously deeper into the crowd. He jumped and jerked. He twirled and tossed. He shivered and shook.

"Broom, Broom! What are you doing? You'll knock me off!" shouted Bohel.

"I'm dancing, Cat! Getting into the spirit of things!" the broom yelled back, and shrugged the kitten off his brush.

"Good-bye, good-bye!" he called, and rocked away into the wreathing smoke and the leaping light.

That was the last Bohel saw of the skinny old broom.

Slipping nimbly through the press of witches and scarecrows, pumpkins and brooms, ghosts of pirates who had walked the plank, wraiths of maidens who'd been imprisoned in towers—weaving through the motley, the merry, the moon-struck mob, Bohel made his way and at length sprang into a tree. In a branch high over the throng he crouched and waited.

He knew no one, now that the broom was gone.

He could only wait here by himself, looking down at the merriment and roistering, hoping to spy, by firelight or moonlight, his mother and father, trusting that they would, somehow, some way, get here despite hindrance or attempts to stop them.

Time passed.

Watching wistfully as the dancers flew round the fire with echoing shrieks of delight, Bohel realized that this was no ragtag orgy but an assemblage of creatures known to one another, celebrating a joyous once-a-year convocation. The air was increasingly rent with clamor and clangor, and Bohel, no stranger to caterwauling himself, looked on with approval. But he did not take part.

He could not take part until—

And then! There! Over to one side, standing at the margin of the great frolic but taking no more part than he was himself, were his very own darling parents after all this time.

There they were!

Father with his pipe, Mother with her squashy pot holder. They stood looking into the melee, as if without hope. And here he was, their kitten and pride, waiting for them!

With a yowl of utter and matchless joy, Bohel

dropped out of the tree onto his father's shoulder.

Oh, what a reunion was this little one in the midst of the great reunion! How the scarecrows patted and petted and hugged their son close! How he mewed into their ears his tale of loneliness and longing!...

After a long time of reassuring—each to the others—they pranced off to join the carousal. Blossom and Handy had never before enjoyed a riot-and-revel as they did this, the first with their own dear child. They watched with pride as he leaped and yowled and arched his back with the other cats.

"How elegantly he capers and cavorts," Blossom said happily. "He's *quite* enchanting."

"He's remarkable," Handy agreed. "You'd think he'd been a coven creature for years." He turned and bowed to his wife.

"Now, my dear, that we're all together again, may I have this dance with you?"

Nine

The light of the rising sun was a glow upon the hilltops before the party ended and the vast eerie company disappeared. The fire was a wan circle of ash, the jack-o'-lanterns' fiery smiles were eclipsed. Ghosts and wraiths melted away, witches mounted their brooms and flew off soundlessly.

Bohel looked around for his broom, but the clearing was empty. Perhaps he'd found another witch to join him. Bohel hoped so. He hoped that, tipsy as the broom had been, he had not fallen into the fire.

"The broom's gone that I came with," he said to his parents.

"Of course," said his father. "No one stays when the party is over."

Blossom added contentedly, "Over for *this* year."

"Tell me now what happened to you," the kitten said. He'd asked this of them several times during the festivities on the hill, but his parents had been too busy dancing and greeting friends to answer him.

"Wait till we get home," said Handy. "We'll tell you all about it then."

"Home!" said Blossom. "I wondered if we would ever see our little boy or our horse stall again. Oh, I think I have never been so happy before in my life."

Handy reached over and gently patted his son's head. "Together again," he murmured, his voice low with fatigue and contentment.

In the afternoon, when Blossom and Handy had had a good rest, the three of them sat outside the barn while Bohel learned of the terrible time his parents had come through so bravely.

"You see," Handy said, "there was nothing we could do when that young couple abducted us. They took us to their house and put us in the sleigh on their front lawn. For a Hallowe'en decoration! What an indignity!"

"Oh, I don't know," said Blossom. "Now that

it's over, I think it was sort of fun. All their friends said we were simply marvelous, sitting there surrounded with apples and stalks of corn.''

"I expect we *did* look pretty handsome,'' said Handy. "As you say, now that it's over, we can say it wasn't so bad. While it was going on, it could not have been worse. I was so worried about you, Bohel, and couldn't stop wondering how you'd feel when you found us gone.''

"Yes,'' said Blossom. "That was the awful part—wondering about you.''

"I was frightened and lonely,'' said Bohel. "And what *I* couldn't stop wondering was if I'd ever see you again.''

They sat in silence, in profound thankfulness that they were here, together once again.

"They did say,'' Blossom went on after a while, "that we could stay in the sleigh on the lawn through Thanksgiving. It *would* be a job, after all.''

"I suppose we have to consider that,'' said Handy.

"Why?'' asked Bohel.

His father and mother stared at him in astonishment.

"My goodness," exclaimed Blossom.

"Bohel," said Handy, "you have put your paw on it once again. Why should we go back there to work? Or anywhere else to work? What do we need that we don't have?"

"We have our son," said Blossom. "We have *each other*. We have our little garden and a roof over our heads. You have your corncob pipe, Handy, and I have my lovely pot holder. I simply don't see what else we could want, or even use."

Bohel, who didn't require even a pipe or a pot holder to make his life complete, purred as he tidied his nails and his tail.

So the big job hunt was over, and the scarecrows and their child settled down just to being together.

THE END

Well, not quite THE END.

Everyone (except kittens) knows that kittens grow up to be cats, and Bohel was no exception. The day came when he was obliged by nature and the way things are to leave his mother and father and go out into the world on his own.

Of course, they all meet and dance together every year at Hallowe'en.

As for Blossom and her husband, Handforth, they still live in the horse stall, planting their garden, sitting together against the barn wall as evening falls, talking over olden times, of years when they exchanged glances over the garden fence, of the day when Handy stumped across the field to declare his love, of Bohel's kittenhood and their happiness then.

They hold hands and smile at each other, because they are happy still.

They enjoy 364 days of quiet, and one night of carousal.

THE END